The Child of Pleasure
Book III

by

Gabriele D'Annunzio

The Child of Pleasure
Book III
by Gabriele D'Annunzio

Copyright © 2024

All Rights reserved.

ISBN: 978-93-63055-39-1

Published by

DOUBLE 9 BOOKS

2/13-B, Ansari Road
Daryaganj, New Delhi – 110002
info@double9books.com
www.double9books.com
Tel. 011-40042856

ABOUT THE AUTHOR

Gabriele D'Annunzio was a notable figure in Italian literature from 1889 to 1910, and in politics from 1914 to 1924. He was frequently referred to as il Vate ("the Poet"; the Italian vate derives from Latin vates and means a poet with a specific emphasis on prophetic, inspiring, or divining abilities) and il Profeta ("the Prophet"). D'Annunzio's literary works were affiliated with the Decadent movement, which was closely related to French symbolism and British aestheticism. Such works signified a departure from the naturalism of the previous romantics, and were both sensual and mystical. He was influenced by Friedrich Nietzsche, which he expressed through his creative and subsequently political efforts. During the Great combat, D'Annunzio's reputation in Italy shifted from literary icon to national combat hero. He was linked with the elite Arditi storm soldiers of the Italian Army and participated in actions such as the Flight over Vienna. As part of an Italian nationalist reaction to the 1919 Paris Peace Conference, he established the short-lived Italian Regency of Carnaro near Fiume, naming himself Duce. The Carnaro Charter established music as a basic principle of the corporatist state. Although D'Annunzio later espoused nationalism and never referred to himself as a fascist, he is recognized with partially establishing Italian fascism, as both his ideas and aesthetics influenced Benito Mussolini.

CONTENTS

CHAPTER I

Two or three days after the departure of the Ferrès, Sperelli and his cousins returned to Rome, Donna Francesca, contrary to her custom, wishing to shorten her stay at Schifanoja.

After a brief stay at Naples, Andrea reached Rome on the 24th of October, a Sunday, in the first heavy morning rain of the Autumn season. He experienced an extraordinary pleasure in returning to his apartments in the Casa Zuccari, his tasteful and charming *buen retiro*. There he seemed to find again some portion of himself, something he had missed. Nothing was altered; everything about him retained, in his eyes, that indescribable look of life which material objects assume, amongst which one has lived and loved and suffered. His old servants, Jenny and Terenzio, had taken the utmost care of everything, and Stephen had attended to every detail likely to conduce to his master's comfort.

It was raining. Andrea went to the window and stood for some time looking out upon his beloved Rome. The piazza of the Trinità de' Monti was solitary and deserted, left to the guardianship of its obelisk. The trees along the wall that joins the church to the Villa Medici, already half stripped of their leaves, rustled mournfully in the wind and the rain. The Pincio alone still shone green, like an island in a lake of mist.

And as he gazed, one sentiment dominated all the others in his heart; the sudden and lively re-awakening of his old love for Rome—fairest Rome— that city of cities, immense, imperial, unique—like the sea, for ever young, for ever new, for ever mysterious.

'What time is it?' Andrea asked of Stephen.

It was about nine o'clock. Feeling somewhat tired, he determined to have a sleep: also, that he would see no one that day and spend the evening quietly at home. Seeing that he was about to re-enter the life of the great world of Rome, he wished, before taking up the old round of activity, to indulge in a little meditation, a slight preparation; to lay down certain rules, to discuss with himself his future line of conduct.

'If any one calls,' he said to Stephen, 'say that I have not yet returned; and let the porter know it too. Tell James I shall not want him to-day, but he can come round for orders this evening. Bring me lunch at three—something very light—and dinner at nine. That is all.'

He fell asleep almost immediately. The servant woke him at two and informed him that, just before twelve o'clock, the Duke of Grimiti had called, having heard from the Marchesa d'Ateleta that he had returned to town.

'Well?'

'Il Signor Duca left word that he would call again in the afternoon.'

'Is it still raining? Open the shutters wide.'

The rain had stopped, the sky was lighter. A band of pale sunshine streamed into the room and spread over the tapestry representing *The Virgin with the Holy Child and Stefano Sperelli,* a work of art brought by Giusto Sperelli from Flanders in 1508. Andrea's eyes wandered slowly over the walls, rejoicing in the beautiful hangings, the harmonious tints; and all these things so familiar and so dear to him seemed to offer him a welcome. The sight of them afforded him intense pleasure, and then the image of Maria Ferrès rose up before him.

He raised himself a little on the pillows, lit a cigarette and abandoned himself luxuriously to his meditations. An unwonted sense of comfort and well-being filled his body, while his mind was in its happiest vein. His thoughts mingled with the rings of smoke in the subdued light in which all forms and colours assume a pleasing vagueness.

Instead of reverting to the days that were past, his thoughts carried him forward into the future.—He would see Donna Maria again in two or three months—perhaps much sooner; there was no saying. Then he would resume the broken thread of that love which held for him so many obscure promises, so many secret attractions. To a man of culture, Donna Maria Ferrès was the Ideal Woman, Baudelaire's *Amie avec des hanches,* the perfect *Consolatrix,* the friend who can hold out both comfort and pardon. Though she had marked those sorrowful lines in the volume of Shelley, she had, most assuredly, said very different words in her heart. 'I can never be thine!' Why *never*? Ah, there had been too much passionate intensity for that in the voice in which she answered him that day in the wood at Vicomile—'I love you! I love you! I love you!'

He could hear her voice now, that never-to-be-forgotten voice!

Stephen knocked at the door. 'May I remind the Signor Conte that it is three o'clock?'

Andrea rose and passed into the octagonal room to dress. The sun shone through the lace window screens and sparkled on the Hispano-Mauresque tiles, the innumerable toilet articles of crystal and silver, the bas-reliefs on the antique sarcophagus; its dancing reflections imparting a delightful sense of movement to the air. He felt in the best of spirits, completely cured, full of the joy and the vivacity of life. He was inexpressibly happy to be back in his home once more. All that was most frivolous, most capricious, most worldly in him awoke with a bound. It was as if the surrounding objects had the power to evoke in him the man of former days. His sensual curiosity, his elasticity, his ubiquity of mind reappeared. He already began to feel the necessity of expansion, of mixing in the world of pleasure and with his friends.

He discovered that he was very hungry, and ordered the servant to bring the lunch at once. He rarely dined at home, but for special occasions—some *recherché* lunch or private little supper—he had a dining-room decorated with eighteenth century Neapolitan tapestries which Carlo Sperelli had ordered of Pietro Dinanti in 1766 from designs by Storace. The seven wall panels represented episodes of Bacchic love, the portières and the draperies above the doors and windows having groups of fruit and flowers. Shades of gold—pale or tawny—predominated, and mingling with the warm, pearly flesh-tints and sombre blues, formed a harmony of colour that was both delicate and sumptuous.

'When the Duke of Grimiti comes back, show him up,' he said to the servant.

Into this room too, the sun, sinking towards the Monte Mario, shot his dazzling rays. You could hear the rumble of the carriages in the piazza of the Trinità de' Monti. The rain over, it looked as if all the luminous gold of the Roman October were spread out over the city.

'Open the window,' he said to the servant.

The noise of the carriage wheels was louder now, a soft damp breeze stirred the curtains lightly.

'Divine Rome!' he thought as he looked at the sky between the wide curtains.

An irresistible curiosity drew him to the open window.

Rome appeared, all pearly gray, spread out before him, its lines a little blurred like a faded picture, under a Claude Lorrain sky, sprinkled with ethereal clouds, their noble grouping lending to the clear spaces between an indescribable delicacy, as flowers lend a new grace to the verdure which surrounds them. On the distant heights the gray deepened gradually to amethyst. Long trailing vapours slid through the cypresses of the Monte Mario like waving locks through a comb of bronze. Close by, the pines of the Monte Pincio spread their sun-gilded canopies. Below, on the piazza, the obelisk of Pius vi. looked like a pillar of agate. Under this rich autumnal light everything took on a sumptuous air.

Divine Rome!

He feasted his eyes on the prospect before him. Looking down, he saw a group of red-robed clerics pass along by the church; then the black coach of a prelate with its two black, long-tailed horses; then other open carriages containing ladies and children. He recognised the Princess of Ferentino with Barbarella Viti, followed by the Countess of Lucoli driving a pair of ponies and accompanied by her great Danish hound. A perturbing breath of the old life passed over his spirit, awakening indeterminate desires in his heart.

He left the window and returned to his lunch. The sun shone on the wall and lit up a dance of satyrs round a Silenus.

'The Duke of Grimiti and two other gentlemen,' announced the servant.

The Duke entered with Ludovico Barbarisi and Giulio Musellaro. Andrea hastened forward to meet them and they greeted him warmly.

'You, Giulio!' exclaimed Sperelli, who had not seen his friend for more than two years. How long have you been in Rome?'

'Only a week. I was going to write to you to Schifanoja, but thought I would rather wait till you came back. And how are you? You are looking a little thin, but very well. It was only when I got back to Rome that I heard of your affair; otherwise, I would certainly have come from India to offer you my services. At the beginning of May, I was at Padmavati in the Bahara. What a heap of things I have to tell you!'

'And so have I!'

They shook hands heartily a second time. Sperelli seemed overjoyed. None of his friends were so dear to him as Musellaro, for his noble character, his keen and penetrating mind and rare culture.

'Ruggiero—Ludovico—sit down. Giulio, will you sit here?'

He offered them tea, cigarettes, liqueurs. The conversation grew very lively. Grimiti and Barbarisi gave the news of Rome, especially the more spicy items of society gossip. The aroma of the tea mingled with that of the tobacco.

'I have brought you a chest of tea,' said Musellaro to Sperelli, 'and much better tea too than your famous Kien Loung used to drink.'

'Ah, do you remember, in London, how he used to make tea after the poetical method of the Great Emperor?'

'I say,' said Grimiti, 'do you know that the fair Clara Green is in Rome? I saw her on Sunday at the Villa Borghese. She recognised me and stopped her carriage to speak to me. She is as lovely as ever. You remember her passion for you, and how she went on when she thought you were in love with Constance Landbrooke? She instantly asked for news of you.'

'I should be very pleased to see her again. Does she still dress in green and wear sunflowers in her hat?

'Oh no. She has apparently abandoned the æsthetic for good and all. She goes in for feathers now. On Sunday, she was wearing an enormous hat à la Montpensier with a perfectly fabulous feather in it.'

'The season is in full swing, I suppose?'

'Earlier than usual this year, both as to saints and sinners.'

'Which of the saints are already in Rome?'

'Almost all—Giulia Moceto, Barbarella Viti, the Princess of Micigliano, Laura Miano, the Marchesa Massa d'Alba, the Countess Lucoli——'

'I saw her just now from the window, driving. And I saw your cousin too with Barbarella Viti.'

'My cousin is only here till to-morrow, then she goes back to Frascati. On Wednesday, she gives a kind of garden party at the villa in the style of the Princess of Sagan. Costume is not absolutely *de rigueur*, but the ladies will all wear Louis xv. or Directoire hats. We are going.'

'You are not leaving Rome again so soon, I hope?' Grimiti asked of Sperelli.

'I shall stay till the beginning of November. Then I am going to France for a fortnight to see about some horses. I shall be back in Rome about the end of the month.'

'Talking of horses,' said Ludovico, 'Leonetto Lanza wants to sell *Campomorto*. You know it—a magnificent animal, a first-rate jumper. That would be something for you.'

'How much does he want for it?'

'Fifteen thousand lire, I think.'

'Well, we might see — —'

'Leonetto is going to be married directly. He got engaged this summer at Aix-les-Bains.'

'I forgot to tell you,' said Musellaro, 'that Galeazzo Secinaro sends you his remembrances. We travelled back from India together. If you only knew of all Galeazzo's doughty deeds on the journey! He is at Palermo now, but he will be in Rome in January.'

'And Gino Bomminaco begs to be remembered to you,' added Barbarisi.

'Ah, ha!' exclaimed the duke with a burst of laughter, 'you should get Gino to tell you the story of his adventure with Donna Giulia Moceto. You are, I fancy, in a position to give us some details on the subject of Donna Giulia.'

Ludovico, too, began to laugh.

'Oh, I know,' broke in Musellaro, 'you have made the most tremendous conquests in Rome. *Gratulator tibi!*'

'But tell me—do tell me about this adventure,' asked Andrea with impatient curiosity.

These subjects excited him. Encouraged by his friends, he launched forth into a discourse on female beauty, displaying the profound knowledge and fervour of a connoisseur, taking a pleasure in using the most highly-coloured expressions, with the subtle distinctions of an artist and a libertine. Indeed, had any one taken the trouble to write down the conversation of the four young men within these walls, hung with the voluptuous scenes of the Bacchic tapestries, it might well have formed the *Breviarium arcanum* of upper-class corruption at the end of the nineteenth century.

The shades of evening were falling, but the air was still permeated with light as a sponge absorbs the water. Through the windows, one caught a glimpse of the horizon and a band of orange against which the cypresses of the Monte Mario stood out sharply like the teeth of a great ebony rake. Ever and anon, came the cawing of the rooks, assembling in groups on the roof of the Villa Medici before descending on the Villa Borghese and into the narrow Valley of Sleep.

'What are you going to do this evening?' Barbarisi asked Andrea.

'I really don't know.'

'Well, then, come with us—dinner at eight, at Doney's, to inaugurate his new restaurant at the Teatro Nazionale.'

'Yes, come with us, do come with us!' entreated Giulio Musellaro.

'Besides the three of us,' continued the duke, 'there will be Giulia Arici, Bébé Silva and Maria Fortuna—That reminds me—capital idea!—you bring Clara Green.'

'A capital idea!' echoed Ludovico Barbarisi.

'And where shall I find Clara Green?'

'At the Hotel de l'Europe, close by, in the Piazza di Spagna. A note from you would put her in the seventh heaven. She is certain to give up any other engagement she may have.'

Andrea was quite agreeable to the plan.

'But it would be better if I called on her,' he said. 'She is pretty sure to be in now. Don't you think so, Ruggiero?'

'Well, dress quick and come out with us now.'

Clara Green had just come in. She received Andrea with childish delight. No doubt she would have preferred to dine alone with him, but she accepted the invitation without hesitating, wrote a note to excuse herself from a previous engagement, and sent the key of her box at the theatre to a lady friend. She seemed overjoyed. She told him a string of sentimental stories and vowed that she had never been able to forget him; holding Andrea's hands in hers while she talked.

I love you more than words can say, Andrew:

She was still young. With her pure and regular profile, her pale gold hair parted and knotted very low on her neck, she looked like a beauty in a Keepsake. A certain affectation of æstheticism clung to her since her liaison with the poet-painter Adolphus Jeckyll, a disciple in poetry of Keats, in painting of Holman Hunt; a composer of obscure sonnets, a painter of subjects from the *Vita Nuova*. She had sat to him for a *Sibylla Palmifera* and a *Madonna with the Lily*. She had also sat to Andrea for a study of the head of Isabella in Boccaccio's story. Art therefore had conferred upon her the stamp of nobility. But, at bottom, she possessed no spiritual qualities whatsoever; she even became tiresome in the long-run by reason of that sentimental romanticism so often affected by English *demi-mondaines* which contrasts so strangely with the depravity of their licentiousness.

'Who would have thought that we should ever be together again, Andrew?'

An hour later, Andrea left her and returned to the Palazzo Zuccari by the little flight of steps leading from the Piazza Mignanelli to the Trinità.

The murmur of the city floated up the solitary little stairway through the mild air of the October evening. The stars twinkled in a cool pure sky. Down below, at the Palazzo Casteldelfina, the shrubs inside the little gate cast vague uncertain shadows in the mysterious light, like marine plants waving at the bottom of an aquarium. From the palace, through a lighted window with red curtains, came the tinkle of a piano. The church bells were ringing. Andrea felt his heart suddenly grow heavy. The recollection of Donna Maria came back to him with a rush, filling him with a dim sense of regret, almost of remorse. What was she doing at this moment? Thinking? Suffering? Deep sadness fell upon him. He felt as if something in the depths of his heart had taken flight—he could not define what it was, but it affected him as some irreparable loss.

He thought of his plan of the morning—an evening of solitude in the rooms to which some day perhaps she might come, an evening, sad yet sweet, in company with remembrances and dreams, in company with her spirit, an evening of meditation and self-communings. In truth, he had kept well to his promises! He was on his way to a dinner with friends and *demi-mondaines* and, doubtless, would go home with Clara Green afterwards.

His regret was so poignant, so intolerable, that he dressed with unwonted rapidity, jumped into his brougham and arrived at the hotel before the appointed time. He found Clara ready and waiting, and offered her a drive round the streets of Rome to pass the time till eight o'clock.

They drove through the Via del Babuino, round the obelisk in the Piazza del Popolo, along the Corso and to the right down the Via della Fontanella di Borghese, returning by the Montecitorio to the Corso which they followed as far as the Piazza di Venezia and so to the Teatro Nazionale. Clara kept up an incessant chatter, bending, every other minute, towards her companion to press a kiss on the corner of his mouth, screening the furtive caress behind a fan of white feathers which gave out a delicate odour of 'white rose.' But Andrea appeared not to hear her, and even her caress only drew from him a slight smile.

'*Che pensi?*' she asked, pronouncing the Italian words with a certain hesitation which was very taking.

'Nothing,' returned Andrea, taking up one of her ungloved hands and examining the rings.

'*Chi lo sa!*' she sighed, throwing a vast amount of expression into these three words, which foreign women pick up at once, because they imagine that they contain all the pensive melancholy of Italian love. '*Chi lo sa!*'

With a sudden change of humour, Andrea kissed her on the ear, slipped an arm round her waist and proceeded to say a host of foolish things to her. The Corso was very lively, the shop windows resplendent, newspaper-vendors yelled, public and private vehicles crossed the path of their carriage; all the stir and animation of Roman evening life was in full swing from the Piazza Colonna to the Piazza di Venezia.

It was ten minutes past eight by the time they reached Doney's. The other guests were already there. Andrea Sperelli greeted the assembled company, and taking Clara Green by the hand—

'This,' he said, 'is Miss Clara Green, *ancilla Domini, Sibylla palmifera, candida puella.*'

'*Ora pro nobis!*' replied Musellaro, Barbarisi, and Grimiti in chorus.

The women laughed though they did not understand. Clara smiled, and slipping out of her cloak appeared in a white dress, quite simple and short, with a V-shaped opening back and front, a knot of sea-green ribbon on her left shoulder, and emeralds in her ears, perfectly unabashed by the triple scrutiny of Giulia Arici, Bébé Silva and Maria Fortuna.

Musellaro and Grimiti were old acquaintances; Barbarisi was introduced.

Andrea proceeded—'Mercedes Silva, surnamed Bébé—*chica pero qualsa.*

'Maria Fortuna, a veritable *Fortuna publica* for our Rome which has the good fortune to possess her.'

Then, turning to Barbarisi—'Do us the honour to present us to this lady who is, if I am not mistaken, the divine Giulia Farnese.'

'No—Arici,' Giulia broke in.

'Oh, I beg your pardon, but really, to believe that, I should have to call upon all my powers of credulity and to consult Pinturicchio in the Fifth Room.'

He uttered these absurdities with a grave smile, amusing himself by bewildering and teasing these pretty fools. In the *demi-monde* he adopted a manner and style entirely his own, using grotesque phrases, launching the most ridiculous paradoxes or atrocious impertinences under cover of the ambiguity of his words; and all this in most original language, rich in a thousand different flavours, like a Rabelaisian *olla podrida* full of strong spices and succulent morsels.

'Pinturicchio,' asked Giulia turning to Barbarisi; 'who's that?'

'Pinturicchio,' exclaimed Andrea, 'oh, a sort of feeble house-painter who once took it into his head to paint your picture on a door in the Pope's apartments. Never mind him—he is dead.'

'Dead? How?'

'In a most appalling manner! His wife's lover was a soldier from Perugia in garrison at Sienna—ask Ludovico—he knows all about it, but has never liked to tell you, for fear of hurting your feelings. Allow me to inform you, Bébé, that the Prince of Wales does not begin to smoke till between the second and third courses—never sooner. You are anticipating.'

Bébé Silva had lighted a cigarette and was eating oysters, while she let the smoke curl through her nostrils. She was like a restless schoolboy, a little depraved hermaphrodite; pale and thin, the brightness of her eyes heightened by fever and kohl, with lips that were too red, and short and rather woolly hair that covered her head like an astrachan cap. Fixed tightly in her left eye was a single eye-glass; she wore a high stiff collar, a white necktie, an open waistcoat, a little black coat of masculine cut and a gardenia in her button-hole. She affected the manners of a dandy and spoke in a deep husky voice. And just therein lay the secret of her attraction—in this imprint of vice, of depravity, of abnormity in her appearance, her attitudes and her words. *Sal y pimienta.*

Maria Fortuna, on the contrary, was of somewhat bovine type, a Madame de Parabère with a tendency to stoutness.

Like the fair mistress of the Regent, she possessed a very white skin, one of those opaque white complexions which seem only to flourish and improve on sensual pleasure. Her liquid violet eyes swam in a faint blue shadow; and her lips, always a little parted, disclosed a vague gleam of pearl behind their soft rosy line, like a half-opened shell.

Giulia Arici took Andrea's fancy very much on account of her golden-brown tints and her great velvety eyes of that soft deep chestnut that sometimes shows tawny gleams. The somewhat fleshy nose, and the full, dewy scarlet, very firm lips gave the lower part of her face a frankly animal look. Her eye-teeth, which were too prominent, raised her upper lip a little and she continually ran the point of her tongue along the edge to moisten it, like the thick petal of a rose running over a row of little white almonds.

'Giulia,' said Andrea with his eyes on her mouth, 'Saint Bernard uses, in one of his sermons, an epithet which would suit you marvellously. And I'll be bound you don't know this either.'

Giulia laughed her sonorous rather vacant laugh, exhaling, in the excitement of her hilarity, a more poignant perfume, like a scented shrub when it is shaken.

'What will you give me,' continued Andrea, 'if I extract from the holy sermon a voluptuous motto to fit you?'

'I don't know,' she replied laughing, holding a glass of Chablis in her long slender fingers. 'Anything you like.'

'The substantive of the adjective.'

'What?'

'We will come back to that presently. The word is: *linguatica*—Messer Ludovico, you can add this clause to your litanies—'*Rosa linguatica, glube nos.*'

'What a pity,' said Musellaro, 'that you are not at the table of a sixteenth-century prince, sitting between a Violante and an Imperia with Pietro Aretino, Giulio Romano, and Marc' Antonio!'

CHAPTER II

The year was dying gracefully. A late wintry sun filled the sky over Rome with a soft, mild, golden light that made the air feel almost spring-like. The streets were full as on a Sunday in May. A stream of carriages passed and repassed rapidly through the Piazza Barberini and the Piazza di Spagna, and from thence a vague and continuous rumble mounted to the Trinità de' Monti and the Via Sistina and even faintly reached the apartments of the Palazzo Zuccari.

The rooms began slowly to fill with the scent exhaled from numberless vases of flowers. Full-blown roses hung their heavy heads over crystal vases that opened like diamond lilies on a golden stem, similar to those standing behind the Virgin in the *tondo* of Botticelli in the Borghese Gallery. No other shape of vase is to be compared with this for elegance; in that diaphanous prison, the flowers seemed to etherealise and had more the air of a religious than an amatory offering.

For Andrea Sperelli was expecting Elena Muti.

He had met her only yesterday morning in the Via Condotti, where she was looking at the shops. She had returned to Rome a day or two before, after her long and mysterious absence. They had both been considerably agitated by the unexpected encounter, but the publicity of the street compelled them to treat one another with ceremonious, almost cold politeness. However, he had said with a grave, half-mournful air, looking her full in the eyes—'I have much to say to you, Elena; will you come to my rooms to-morrow? Everything is just as it used to be—nothing is changed.' To which she replied quite simply—'Very well, I will come. You may expect me about four o'clock. I too have something to say to you—but leave me now.'

That she should have accepted the invitation so promptly, without demur, without imposing any conditions or seemingly attaching the smallest importance to the matter, roused a certain vague suspicion in Andrea's mind. Was she coming as friend or lover?—to renew old ties or to destroy all hope of such a thing for ever? What vicissitudes had not occurred in this woman's soul during the last two years? Of that he was necessarily ignorant, but he had carried away with him the thrill of emotion called up in him by Elena's glance when they suddenly met in the street and he bent his head in greeting before her. It was the same look as of old—so tender, so deep, so infinitely seductive from under the long lashes.

Everything in the arrangement of the rooms showed evidences of special loving care. Logs of juniper wood burned brightly on the hearth; the little tea-table stood ready with its cups and saucers of Castel-Durante majolica, of antique shape and inimitable grace, whereon were depicted mythological subjects by Luzio Dolci, with lines from Ovid underneath in black characters and a running hand. The light from the windows was tempered by heavy curtains of red brocade embroidered all over with silver pomegranates, trailing leaves and mottos. The declining sun, as it caught the window-panes, cast the shadow of the lace blinds on the carpet.

The clock of the Trinità struck half-past three. He had half an hour still to wait. Andrea rose from the sofa where he had been lying and opened one of the windows; he wandered aimlessly about the room, took up a book, read a few lines and threw it down again; looked about him undecidedly as if searching for something. The suspense was so trying that he felt the necessity of rousing himself, of counteracting his mental disquietude by physical means. He went over to the fireplace, stirred up the logs and put on a fresh one. The glowing mass collapsed, sending up a shower of sparks, and part of it rolled out as far as the fender. The flames broke into a quantity of little tongues of blue fire, springing up and disappearing fitfully, while the broken ends of the log smoked.

The sight brought back certain memories to him. In days gone by Elena had been fond of lingering over this fireside. She expended much art and ingenuity in piling the wood high on the fire-dogs, grasping the heavy tongs in both hands and leaning her head slightly back to avoid the sparks. Her hands were small and very supple, with that tendril-like flexibility, so to speak, of a Daphne at the very first onset of the fabled metamorphose.

Scarcely were these matters arranged to her satisfaction than the logs would catch and send forth a sudden blaze, and the warm ruddy light would struggle for a moment with the icy gray shades of evening filtering through the windows. The sharp fumes of the burning wood seemed to rise to her head, and facing the glowing mass Elena would be seized with fits of childish glee. She had a rather cruel habit of pulling all the flowers to pieces and scattering them over the carpet at the end of each of her visits and then stand ready to go, fastening a glove or a bracelet, and smile in the midst of the devastation she had wrought.

Nothing was changed since then. A host of memories were associated with these things which Elena had touched, on which her eyes had rested, and scenes of that time rose up vividly and tumultuously before him. After nearly two years' absence, Elena was going to cross his threshold once more. In half an hour, she would be seated in that chair—a little out of breath at first, as of yore—would have removed her veil—be speaking. All these familiar objects would hear the sound of her voice again—perhaps even her laugh—after two long years.

'How shall I receive her—what shall I say?'

He was quite sincere in his anxiety and nervousness, for he had really begun to love this woman once more, but the expression of his sentiments, whether verbal or otherwise, was ever with him such an artificial matter, so far removed from truth and simplicity, that he had recourse to these preparations from pure habit even when, as was the case now, he was sincerely and deeply moved.

He tried to imagine the scene beforehand, to compose some phrases; he looked about him in the room, considering where would be the most appropriate spot for the interview. Then he went over to a looking-glass to see if his face were as pale as befitted the occasion, and his gaze rested complacently on his forehead, just where the hair began at the temples and where, in the old days, Elena was often wont to press a delicate kiss. In matters of love, his vitiated and effeminate vanity seized upon every advantage of personal grace or of dress to heighten the charm of his appearance, and he knew how to extract the greatest amount of pleasure therefrom. The chief reason of his unfailing success lay in the fact that, in the game of love, he shrank from no artifice, no duplicity, no falsehood that might further his cause. A great portion of his strength lay in his capacity for deception.

'What shall I do—what shall I say when she comes?'

His mind was all undecided and yet the minutes were flying. Besides, he had no idea in what frame of mind Elena might arrive.

It wanted but two or three minutes now to the hour. His excitement was so great that he felt half suffocated. He returned to the window and looked out at the steps of the Trinità. She used always to come up those steps, and when she reached the top, would halt for a moment before rapidly crossing the square in front of the Casa Casteldelfina. Through the silence, he often heard the tapping of her light footsteps on the pavement below.

The clock struck four. The rumble of carriage wheels came up from the Piazza di Spagna and the Pincio. A great many people were strolling under the trees in front of the Villa Medici. Two women seated on a stone bench beside the church were keeping watch over some children playing round the obelisk, which shone rosy red under the sunset, and cast a long, slanting, blue-gray shadow.

The air freshened as the sun sank lower. Farther off, the city stood out golden against the colourless clear sky, which made the cypresses on the Monte Mario look jet black.

Andrea started. A shadow stole up the little flight of steps beside the Casa Casteldelfina leading up from the Piazzetta Mignanelli. It was not Elena; it was some other lady, who slowly turned the corner into the Via Gregoriana.

'What if she did not come at all?' he said to himself as he left the window. Coming away from the colder outside air he felt the warmth of the room all the more cosy, the scent of the burning wood and the roses more piercing sweet, the shadow of the curtains and portières more delightfully mysterious. At that moment the whole room seemed on the alert for the arrival of the woman he loved. He imagined Elena's sensations on entering. It was hardly possible that she should be able to resist the influence of these surroundings, so full of tender memories for her; she would suddenly lose all sense of time and reality, would fancy herself back at one of the old rendezvous, the Elena of those happy days. Since nothing was altered in the *mise-en-scène* of their love, why should their love itself be changed? She must of necessity feel the profound charm of all these things which once upon a time had been so dear to her.

And now the anguish of hope deferred created a fresh torture for him. Minds that have the habit of imaginative contemplation and poetic dreaming attribute to inanimate objects a soul, sensitive and variable as their own, and recognise in all things—be it form or colour, sound or perfume—a transparent symbol, an emblem of some emotion or thought; in every phenomenon and every group of phenomena they claim to discover a psychical condition, a moral significance. At times the vision is so lucid as to produce actual pain in such minds, they feel themselves overwhelmed by the plenitude of life revealed to them and are terrified by the phantom of their own creation.

Thus Andrea saw his own dire distress reflected in the aspect of the objects surrounding him, and as his own fond desires seemed wasting fruitlessly in this protracted expectation, so the erotic essence, so to speak, of the room appeared to be evaporating and exhaling uselessly. In his eyes these apartments in which he had loved and also suffered so much had acquired something of his own sensibility—had not only been witness of his loves, his pleasures, his sorrows, but had taken part in it all. In his memories, every outline, every tint harmonised with some feminine image, was a note in a chord of beauty, an element in an ecstasy of passion. The very nature of his tastes led him to seek for a diversity of enjoyment in his love, and seeing that he set out upon that quest as an accomplished artist and æsthetic it was only natural that he should derive a great part of his delight from the world of external objects. To this fastidious actor the comedy of love was nothing without the scenery.

From that point of view his stage was certainly quite perfect, and he himself a most adroit actor-manager; for he almost always entered heart and soul into his own artifice, he forgot himself so completely that he was deceived by his own deception, fell into the trap of his own laying, and wounded himself with his own weapons—a magician enclosed in the spells of his own weaving.

The roses in the tall Florentine vases, they too were waiting and breathing out their sweetness. On the divan cover and on the walls inscriptions on silver scrolls singing the praises of woman and of wine gleamed in the rays of the setting sun, and harmonised admirably with the faded colours of the sixteenth century Persian carpet. Elsewhere the shadow was deeply transparent and as if animated by that indefinable luminous tremor felt in hidden sanctuaries where some mystic treasure lies enshrined. The fire crackled on the hearth, each flame, as Shelley puts it, like a separate jewel dissolved in ever moving light. To Andrea it seemed that at that moment every shape, every colour, every perfume gave forth the essential and delicate spirit of its being. And yet *she* came not, *she* came not!

For the first time, the thought of her husband presented itself to him.

Elena was no longer free. Some months after her abrupt departure from Rome, she had renounced the agreeable liberty of widowhood to marry an English nobleman, Lord Humphrey Heathfield. Andrea had seen the announcement of the marriage in a society paper in the October following and had heard a world of comment on the new Lady Humphrey in every country house he stayed in during the autumn. He remembered also having met Lord Humphrey some half a score of times during the preceding winter at the Saturdays of the Princess Giustiniani-Bandini, or in the public sale-rooms. He was a man of about forty, with colourless fair hair, bald at the temples, an excessively pale face, a pair of piercing light eyes and a prominent forehead, on which a network of veins stood out. He had his name of Heathfield from that lieutenant-general who was the hero of the defence of Gibraltar and afterwards immortalised by the brush of Sir Joshua Reynolds.

What part had this man in Elena's life? What ties, beyond the convention of marriage, bound her to him? What transformations had the physical and moral contact of this husband brought to pass in her?

These enigmas rose tumultuously before him, making his pain so intolerable, that he started up with the instinctive bound of a man who has been stabbed unawares. He crossed the room to the ante-chamber and listened at the door which he had left ajar. It was on the stroke of a quarter to five.

The next moment he heard footsteps on the stair, the rustle of skirts and a quick panting breath. A woman was coming up hurriedly. His heart beat with such vehemence that—his nerves all unstrung by his long suspense—he felt hardly able to stand on his feet. The steps drew nearer, there was a long-drawn sigh—a step upon the landing—at the door—Elena entered.

'O Elena—at last!'

There was in that cry such a profound accent of agony endured, that it brought to Elena's lips an indescribable smile, mingled of pleasure and pity. He took her by her ungloved right hand and drew her into the room. She was still a little out of breath, and under her black veil a faint flush diffused itself over her whole face.

'Forgive me, Andrea! I could not get away any sooner—there is so much to do—so many calls to return—such tiring days! I hardly know where to turn. How warm it is in here! What a delicious smell!'

She was standing in the middle of the room—a little undecided and ill at ease in spite of her rapid and lightly spoken words. A velvet coat with Empire sleeves, very full at the shoulders and buttoned closely at the wrists and with an immense collar of blue fox for sole trimming, covered her from head to foot, but without disguising the grace of her figure. She looked at Andrea with eyes in which a curious tremulous smile softened the flash and sparkle.

'You have changed somehow,' she said; 'I don't quite know what it is—but round your mouth, for instance, there are bitter lines that used not to be there.'

She spoke in a tone of affectionate familiarity. The sound of her voice once more in this room caused him such exquisite delight that he exclaimed—'Speak again, Elena—go on speaking!'

She laughed. 'Why?' she asked.

'You know why,' he answered, taking her hand again.

She drew her hand away and looked the young man deep in the eyes. 'I know nothing any more.'

'Then you have changed very much.'

'Yes—very much indeed.'

They had both dropped their bantering tone. Elena's answer threw a sudden search-light upon much that was problematical before. Andrea understood, and with that rapid and precise intuition so often found in minds practised in psychological analysis, he instantly divined the moral attitude of his visitor, and foresaw the further development of the coming scene. Moreover, he was already under the spell of this woman's fascination as in the former days, besides being greatly piqued by curiosity.

'Will you not sit down?' he asked.

'Yes—for a moment.'

'Here—in this arm-chair.'

'Ah—*my* arm-chair!' she was on the point of exclaiming, for she recognised an old friend, but she stopped herself in time.

The chair was deep and roomy, and covered with antique leather on which pale dragons ramped in relief, after the style of the wall decorations of one of the rooms in the Chigi palace. The leather had taken on that warm and sumptuous tone which recalls the background of certain Venetian portraits, or a fine bronze still retaining traces of former gilding, or a piece of tortoise-shell with gleams of gold here and there. A great cushion covered with a piece of a dalmatic of faded colouring—of that peculiar shade which the Florentine silk merchants used to call 'rosa di gruogo,' saffron red, contributed to its inviting easiness.

Elena seated herself in it, placing on the tea-table beside her her right hand glove and her card-case, a fragile toy in polished silver with a device and motto engraven on it. She then proceeded to remove her veil, raising her arms high to unfasten the knot, her graceful attitude throwing gleams of changeful light on the velvet of her coat, along the sleeves and over the contour of her bust. The heat of the fire was very strong, and with her bare hand, which shone transparent like rosy alabaster, she screened her face from it. The rings on her fingers glittered in the firelight.

'Please screen the fire,' she said, 'it is really too fierce.'

'What—have you lost your fondness for the flames?—and you used to be a perfect salamander. This hearth is full of memories——'

'Let memory sleep,—do not stir the embers,' she interrupted him. 'Screen the fire and let us have some light. I will make the tea.'

'Won't you take off your coat?'

'No, I must go directly—it is late.'

'But you will be melted.'

She rose with a little gesture of impatience. 'Very well then—help me, please.'

As he helped her off with the mantle, Andrea noticed that the scent was not the same as the familiar one of old. However, it was so delicious that it thrilled his every sense.

'You have a new scent,' he said with peculiar emphasis.

'Yes,' she answered simply, 'do you like it?'

Andrea still held the mantle in his hands. He buried his face in the fur collar which had been next her throat and her hair—'What is it called?' he inquired.

'It has no name.'

She re-seated herself in the arm-chair within the circle of the firelight. Her dress was of black lace, on which sparkled a mass of tiny jet and steel beads.

The day was fading from the windows. Andrea lit candles of twisted orange-coloured wax in wrought-iron candlesticks, after which he drew a screen before the fire.

During this pause, both felt a certain perplexing uneasiness; Elena was no longer exactly conscious of the moment, nor was she quite mistress of herself. In spite of all her efforts she was unable to recall with precision her motives for coming here, to follow out her intentions—even to regain her force of will. In the presence of this man to whom, once upon a time, she had been bound by such passionate ties, and in this spot where she lived the most ardent moments of her life, she felt her reserve melting, her mind wavering and growing feeble. She was at that dangerously delicious point of sentiment at which the soul receives its every impulse, its attitudes, its form from its external surroundings as an aërial vapour from the mutations of the atmosphere. But she checked herself before wholly giving way to it.

'Is that right now?' asked Andrea in a low, almost humble voice.

She smiled without replying. His words had given her inexpressibly keen delight.

She began her delicate manipulations—lit the spirit-lamp under the kettle, opened the lacquer tea-caddy and put the necessary quantity of aromatic leaves into the tea-pot, and finally prepared two cups. Her movements were slow and a little hesitating, as happens when the mind is busied with other things than the occupation of the moment; her exquisite white hands hovered over the cups with the airiness of butterflies, and from her whole lithe form there emanated an indefinable charm which enveloped her lover like a caress.

Seated quite close to her, gazing at her from under his half-closed lids, Andrea drank in the subtle fascination of her presence. Neither of them spoke. Elena, leaning back in the cushions, waited for the water to boil, with her eyes fixed on the blue flame while she absently slipped her rings up and down her fingers, lost in a dream apparently. But it was no dream; it was rather a vague reminiscence, faint, confused and evanescent. All the recollections of the love that was past rose up in her mind, but dimly and uncertain, leaving an indistinct impression, she hardly knew whether of pleasure or of pain. It was like the indefinable perfume of a faded bouquet, in which each separate flower has lost the vivacity proper to its colour and its fragrance, but from which emanates a common perfume wherein all the diverse component elements are indistinguishably blended. She seemed to carry in her heart the last breath of memories already faded, the last trace of joys departed for ever, the last tremor of a happiness that was dead—something akin to a mist from out of which images emerge fitfully without shape or name. She knew not, was it pleasure or pain, but by degrees this mysterious agitation, this nameless disquiet waxed greater and filled her soul with joy and bitterness.

She was silent—withdrawn within herself—for though her heart was full to overflowing, her emotion was pleasurably increased by that silence. Speech would have broken the charm.

The kettle began its low song.

Andrea on a low seat, with his elbow on his knee and his chin in his hand, sat watching the fair woman so intently that Elena, without turning, felt that persistent gaze upon her with a sense of physical discomfort. And while he gazed upon her he thought to himself that she seemed altogether a new woman to him—one who had never been his, whom he had never clasped to his heart.

And in truth, she was even more desirable than in the former days, the plastic enigma of her beauty more obscure and more enthralling. Her head with the low broad forehead straight nose and arched eyebrows—so pure and firm in outline, so classically antique in the modelling—might have come from some Syracusan coin. The expression of the eyes and that of the mouth were in singular contrast, giving her that passionate, ambiguous, almost preternatural look that only one or two master-hands, deeply imbued in all the profoundest corruption of art, have been able to infuse into such immortal types of woman as the Mona Lisa and Nelly O'Brien.

The steam began to escape through the hole in the lid of the kettle, and Elena turned her attention once more to the tea-table. She poured a little water on the leaves; put two lumps of sugar in one of the cups, then poured some more water into the tea-pot and extinguished the lamp; doing it all with a certain fond care, but never once looking in Andrea's direction. By this time her inward agitation had resolved itself into such melting tenderness, that there was a lump in her throat and her eyes filled involuntarily; all her contradictory thoughts, all her trouble and agitation of heart, concentrated themselves in those tears.

A movement of her arm knocked the little silver card-case off the table. Andrea picked it up and examined the device: two true lovers' knots each bearing an inscription in English—*From Dreamland*, and *A Stranger here*.

When he raised his head, Elena offered him the fragrant beverage with a mist of tears before her eyes.

He saw that mist, and, filled with love and gratitude at such an unlooked-for sign of melting, he put down the cup, sank on his knees before her, and seizing her hand pressed his lips passionately to it.

'Elena! Elena!' he murmured, his face close to hers as if he would drink the breath from her lips. His emotion was quite sincere, though some of the things he said were not. He loved her—had always loved her—had never, never, never been able to forget her. On meeting her again, he had felt his passion rekindle with such vehemence that it had given him a kind of shock of terror—as if in one lightning flash he had witnessed the upheaval, the convulsion of his whole life.

'Hush—hush——' said Elena with a look of pain, and turning very pale.

But Andrea went on, still on his knees, fanning the flames of his passion by the images he himself evoked. When she had left him so abruptly, he had felt that the greater and better part of him went with her. Afterwards—— never, never could he tell her all the misery of those days, the agony of regret, the ceaseless, implacable, devouring torture of mind and body. His wretchedness grew and increased daily till it burst all bounds and overwhelmed him utterly. Despair lay in wait for him at every turn. The mere flight of time became an intolerable burden. His regrets were less for the happy days gone by than for those that were passing all profitless for love. Those, at least, had left him a memory, these nothing but profoundest regret—nay, almost remorse. His life was preying upon itself, consumed in secret by the inextinguishable flame of one desire, by the unconquerable distaste to any other form of pleasure. Of all the fiery ardour of his youth nothing now remained to him but a handful of ashes. Sometimes, like a dream that vanishes at dawn, all the past, all the present would fade and fall away from his inner consciousness—like a tale that is told, a useless garment. Then he would remember the past no more, as a man newly risen from a long illness, a convalescent still overcome with stupor. At last he could forget—his tortured soul was sinking gently down to death.——But suddenly, out of the depths of this lethal tranquillity his pain had sprung up afresh, and the fallen idol was re-established higher than ever. She and she alone held every fibre of his heart captive beneath her spells, crushing out his intelligence, keeping the doors of his soul against any other passion, any sorrow, any dream to the end of all time——

He was lying of course, but his words were so fervid, his voice so thrilling, the clasp of his hands so fondly caressing that Elena was profoundly touched.

'Hush,' she said, 'I must not, dare not listen to you—I am yours no longer, I never can be yours again—never. Do not say these things——'

'No—listen——'

'I will not—good-bye—I must go now. Good-bye, Andrea,—it is late—let me go.'

She drew her hands out of the young man's clasp, and, successfully throwing off the dangerous languor that was creeping over her, she prepared to rise.

'Then why did you come?' he asked almost roughly, and preventing her from doing so.

Slight as was the force he used, she frowned. She paused before answering.

'I came,' she said in measured accents and looking her lover full in the eyes—'I came because you asked me. For the sake of the love that was once between us, for the manner in which that love was broken and for the long and unexplained silence of my absence I had not the heart to refuse your invitation. Besides, I wanted to say what I have said: that I am no longer yours—that I never can be again—never. That is what I wanted to tell you, honestly and frankly, to save you and myself all painful disillusionment, all danger or bitterness in the future.—Do you understand?'

Andrea bowed his head almost to her knee in silence. She stroked his hair with a familiar gesture of old.

'And then,' she went on in a voice that thrilled him to the heart's core—'and then—I wanted to tell you—that I love you—love you as much as ever: that you are still the heart of my heart and that I will be the fondest of sisters to you, the best of friends—do you understand?'

Andrea made no reply. She took his head between her hands and raised it, forcing him to look her in the face.

'Do you understand?' she repeated in a still lower, sweeter tone. Her eyes under the shadow of the long lashes were suffused with a pure and tender light, her lips were slightly open and trembling.

'No; you never loved me, and you do not love me now!' Andrea burst out at last, pulling Elena's hands from his temples and drawing away from her, for he was sensible of the fire that was kindling in his veins under the mere gaze of those eyes, and his regret at having lost possession of this fairest of women grew more bitter and poignant than before. 'No, you never loved me. You had the heart to strike your love dead at a blow—treacherously almost—just when it had reached its supremest height. You ran away, you deserted me, left me alone in my bewilderment, my misery, while I was still blinded by your promises. You never loved me—neither then nor now. And now, after such a long absence, so full of mystery, so silent and inexorable, after I have wasted the bloom of my life in cherishing a wound that was dear to me because your hand had dealt it—after so much joy and so much pain, you return to this room, in which every object is replete for us with living memories, and you say to me calmly—"I am yours no longer—good-bye."—Oh no—you do not love me.'

'Oh, you are ungrateful!' she cried, deeply wounded by the young man's incensed tone. 'What do you know of all that has occurred, or of what I have had to go through?—What do you know?'

'I know nothing, and what is more, I do not want to,' Andrea retorted stubbornly, enveloping her in a darkling look in which burned the fever of his desire. 'All I know is that you were mine once—wholly and without reserve, and I know that body and soul I shall never forget it——'

'Be silent!'

'What do I care for your sisterly affection? In spite of yourself you offer it with your eyes full of quite another kind of love, and you cannot touch me without your hands trembling. I have seen that look in your eyes too often, you have too often felt me tremble with passion beneath your hands—I love you!'

Carried away by his own words he grasped her wrists tightly and drew so close to her that she felt his hot breath on her cheek. 'I love you, I tell you—more than ever before,' he went on, slipping an arm about her waist to draw her to his kiss—'Have you forgotten—have you forgotten?'

She pushed him forcibly from her and rose to her feet, trembling in every limb.

'I will not—do you hear?'

But he would not hear. He came towards her with arms outstretched, very pale and determined.

'Could you bear,' she cried turning at bay at last, indignant at his violence, 'could you bear to share me with another?'

She flung the cruel question at him point-blank, without reflection, and now stood looking at her lover with wide open frightened eyes, like one who in self-defence has dealt a blow without measuring his strength, and fears to have struck too deep.

Andrea's frenzy dropped on the instant, and his face expressed such overwhelming pain that Elena was stricken to the heart.

After a moment's silence—'Good-bye!' he said, but that one word contained all the bitterness of the words he refrained from saying.

'Good-bye,' she answered gently, 'forgive me.'

They both felt the necessity of putting an end, at least for that evening, to this perilous conversation. Andrea affected an almost over-strained courtesy. Elena became even gentler, almost humble. A nervous tremor shook her continually.

She took her cloak from the chair and Andrea hastened to assist her. As she did not succeed in finding the armholes, Andrea guided her hand to it but scarcely touched her. He then offered her her hat and veil. 'There is a looking-glass in the next room if you would like——'

'No, thank you.' She went over beside the fireplace, where on the wall hung a quaint little old mirror in a frame surrounded by little figures, carved in so airy and vivacious a style that they seemed rather to be of malleable gold than of wood. It was a charming thing, the work doubtless of some delicate artist of the fifteenth century and designed to reflect the charms of some Mona Amorrosisca or some Laldomine. Many a time in the old happy days Elena had put on her veil in front of this dim, lack lustre mirror. She remembered it again now.

On seeing her reflection rise out of its misty depths she was stirred by a singular emotion. A rush of profound sadness came over her. She did not speak.

All this time Andrea was watching her intently.

Her preparations concluded, she said, 'It must be very late.'

'Not very—about six o'clock, I think.'

'I sent away my carriage. I would be very grateful if you could send for a closed cab for me.'

'Will you excuse me then if I leave you alone for a moment? My servant is out.'

She assented. 'And please tell the man yourself where to go to—the Hotel Quirinal.'

He went out and shut the door behind him. She was alone.

She cast a rapid glance around her, embracing the whole room with an indefinable look that lingered on the vases of flowers. The room seemed to her larger, the ceiling higher than she remembered. She began to feel a little giddy. She did not notice the scent of the flowers any longer, but the atmosphere of the room was close and heavy as in a hot-house. Andrea's image appeared to her in a sort of intermittent flashes—a vague echo of his voice rang in her ears. Was she going to faint?—Oh, the delight of it if she might close her eyes and abandon herself to this languor!

She gave herself a little shake and went over to one of the windows, which she opened, and let the breeze blow in her face. Somewhat revived by this she turned back into the room. The pale flame of the candles sent flickering shadows over the walls. The fire burned low but sufficed to light up in part the pious figures on the screen made of stained glass from a church window. The cup of tea stood where Andrea had laid it down on the table, cold and untouched. The chair cushion retained the impress of the form that had leaned against it. All the objects surrounding her breathed an ineffable melancholy, which condensed itself in a heavy weight upon Elena's heart, till it sank beneath the well nigh insupportable burden.

'*Mio Dio! mio Dio!*'

She wished she could make her escape unseen. A puff of wind inflated the curtains, made the candles flicker, raised a general rustle through the room. She shivered, and almost without knowing what she did, she called—

'Andrea!'

Her own voice—that name in the silence startled her strangely, as if neither voice nor name had come from her lips. Why was Andrea so long in returning? She listened.——There was no sound but the dull deep inarticulate murmur of the city. Not a carriage passed across the piazza of the Trinità de' Monti. As the wind came in strong gusts from time to time, she closed the window, catching a glimpse as she did so of the point of the obelisk, black against the starry sky.

Possibly Andrea had not found a conveyance at once on the Piazza Barberini. She sat herself down to wait on the sofa and tried to calm her foolish agitation, avoiding all heartsearchings and endeavouring to fix her attention on external objects. Her eyes wandered to the figures on the fire-screen, faintly visible by the light of the dying logs. On the mantelpiece a great white rose in one of the vases was dropping its petals softly, languidly, one by one, giving an impression of something subtly feminine and sensuous. The cup-like petals rested delicately on the marble, like flakes of snow.

Ah, how sweet that fragrant snow had been *then*! she thought. Rose-leaves strewed the carpets, the divan, the chairs, and she was laughing, happy in the midst of the devastation, and her happy lover was at her feet— —

A carriage stopped down in the street. She rose and shook her aching head to banish the dull weight that seemed to paralyse her. The next moment, Andrea entered out of breath.

'Forgive me,' he said, 'for keeping you so long, but I could not find the porter, so I went down to the Piazza di Spagna. The carriage is waiting for you.'

'Thanks,' answered Elena with a timid glance at him through her black veil.

He was grave and pale but quite calm.

'I expect my husband to-morrow,' she went on in a low faint voice. 'I will send you a line to let you know when I can see you again.'

'Thank you,' answered Andrea.

'Good-bye then,' she said, holding out her hand.

'Shall I see you down to the street? There is no one there.'

'Yes—come down with me.'

She looked about her a little hesitatingly.

'Have you forgotten anything?' asked Andrea.

She was looking at the flowers, but she answered, 'Ah—yes—my card-case.'

Andrea sprang to fetch it from the table. '*A stranger here*?' he read as he handed it to her.

'*No, my dear, a friend— —*'

Her answer was quick, her voice eager. Then suddenly with a smile peculiarly her own, half imploring, half seductive, a mixture of timidity and tenderness, she said: '*Give me a rose.*'

Andrea went from vase to vase gathering all the roses into one great bunch which he could scarcely hold in his hands—some of them shed their petals.

'They were for you—all of them,' he said without looking at her.

Elena hung her head and turned to go in silence followed by Andrea. They descended the stairs still in silence. He could see the nape of her neck so fair and delicate where the little dark curls mingled with the gray-blue fur.

'Elena!' he cried her name in a low voice, incapable any longer of fighting against the passion that filled his heart to bursting.

She turned round to him with a finger on her lips—a gesture of agonised entreaty—but her eyes burned through the shadow. She hastened her steps, flung herself into the carriage and felt rather than saw him lay the roses in her lap.

'Good-bye! Good-bye!'

And when the carriage turned away she threw herself back exhausted and burst into a passion of sobs, tearing the roses to pieces with her poor frenzied hands.

CHAPTER III

So she had come, she had come! She had re-entered the rooms in which every piece of furniture, every object must retain some memory for her, and she had said—'I am yours no more, can never be yours again, never!' and—'Could you suffer to share me with another?'—Yes, she had dared to fling those words in his face, in that room, in sight of all these things!

A rush of pain—atrocious, immeasurable, made up of a thousand wounds, each distinct from the other and one more piercing than the other, came over him and goaded him to desperation. Passion enveloped him once more in a thousand tongues of fire, re-kindling in him an inextinguishable desire for this woman who belonged to him no more, re-awakening in his memory every smallest detail of past caresses and all the sweet mad doings of those days. And yet through it all, there persisted the strange difficulty in identifying that Elena with the Elena of to-day, who seemed to him altogether another woman, one whom he had never known, never held in his arms. The torture of his senses was such that he thought he must die of it. Impurity crept through his blood like a corroding poison.

The impurity which *then* the winged flame of the soul had covered with a sacred veil, had surrounded with a mystery that was half divine, appeared *now* without the veil and without the mystery as a mere carnal lust, a piece of gross sensuality. He knew that the ardour he had felt to-day in her presence was not Love—had nothing in common with Love—for when she had cried—'Could you suffer to share me with another?'—Why, yes, he could suffer it perfectly.

Nothing therefore—nothing in him had remained intact. Even the memory of his grand passion was now corrupted, sullied, debased. The last spark of hope was extinct. He had reached his lowest level, never to rise again.

He was seized by a terrible and frenzied desire to overthrow the idol that still persistently rose up lofty and enigmatic before his imagination, do what he would to abase it. With cynical cruelty, he set himself to insult, to undermine, to mutilate it. The destructive analysis he had already employed upon himself, he now turned upon Elena. To those dubious problems which, at one time, he had resolutely put away from him, he now sought the answer; of all the suspicions which had formerly presented themselves to him only to disappear without leaving a trace, he now studied the origin, found them justified and obtained their confirmation. But whereas he thought to find relief in this furious work of demolition, he only increased his sufferings, aggravated his malady and deepened his wounds.

What had been the true cause of Elena's departure two years before? There were many conflicting rumours at the time, and again when she married Humphrey Heathfield; but the actual truth of the matter was what he heard, quite by chance, among other scraps of society gossip, from Giulio Musellaro one evening as they left the theatre together, nor did Andrea doubt it for a moment. Donna Elena had been obliged to leave Rome for pecuniary reasons, to work some 'operation' which should extricate her from the serious embarrassments into which her outrageous extravagance had plunged her. The marriage with Humphrey Heathfield, who was Marquis of Mount Saint Michael and Earl of Broadford, and besides possessing a considerable fortune was related to the highest nobility of Great Britain, had saved her from ruin. Donna Elena had managed matters with the utmost adroitness and succeeded marvellously in steering clear of the threatening peril. It was not to be denied that the interval of her three years of widowhood had been none too chaste a prelude to a second marriage—neither chaste nor prudent—nevertheless, there was also no denying that Elena Muti was a great lady— —

'Ah, my boy, a grand creature!' said Musellaro, 'as you very well know.'

Andrea said nothing.

'But take my advice,' his friend went on, throwing away the cigarette which had gone out while he talked, 'do not resume your relations with her. It is the same with love as with tobacco—once out, it will not bear relighting. Let us go and get a cup of tea from Donna Giulia Moceto. They tell me one may go to her house after the theatre—it is never too late.'

They were close by the Palazzo Borghese.

'You can,' answered Andrea, 'I am going home to bed. I am rather tired after to-day's run with the hounds. My regards to Donna Giulia—my blessing go with you!'

Musellaro went up the steps of the palace and Andrea continued on his way past the Borghese fountain towards the Trinità.

It was one of those wonderful January nights, cold and serene, which turn Rome into a city of silver set in a ring of diamonds. The full moon, hanging in mid-sky, shed a triple purity of light, of frost, and of silence.

He walked along in the moonlight like a somnambulist, conscious of nothing but his pain. The last blow had been struck, the idol was shattered, nothing remained standing above the ruins—this was the end!

So it was true—she had never really loved him. She had not scrupled to break with him in order to contract a marriage of convenience. And now she put on the airs of a martyr before him, wrapped herself round with a mantle of conjugal inviolability! A bitter laugh rose to his lips, and then a rush of sullen blind rage against the woman came over him. The memory of his passion went for nothing—all the past was one long fraud, one stupendous, hideous lie; and this man, who throughout his whole life had made a practice of dissimulation and duplicity, was now incensed at the deception of another, was as indignant at it as at some unpardonable backsliding, some inexcusable and inexplicable perfidy. He was quite unable to understand how Elena could have committed such a crime; he denied her all possibility of justification, and rejected the hypothesis of some secret and dire necessity having driven her to sudden flight. He could see nothing but the bare brutal fact, its baseness, its vulgarity—above all its vulgarity, gross, manifest, odious, without one extenuating circumstance. In short, the whole matter reduced itself to this: a passion which was apparently sincere, which they had vowed was profound and inextinguishable, had been broken off for a question of money, for material interests, for a commercial transaction.

'Oh, you are ungrateful! What do you know of all that has happened, of all I have suffered!'

Elena's words recurred to him with everything else she had said, from beginning to end of their interview—her words of fondness, her offer of sisterly affection, all her sentimental phrases. And he remembered, too, the tears that had dimmed her eyes, her changes of countenance, her tremors, her choking voice when she said good-bye, and he laid the roses in her lap. 'But why had she ever consented to come? Why play this part, call up all these emotions, arrange this comedy? Why?

By this time he had reached the top of the steps, and found himself in the deserted piazza. Suddenly the beauty of the night filled him with a vague but desperate yearning towards some unknown good. The image of Maria Ferrès flashed across his mind; his heart beat fast, he thought of what it would be to hold her hands in his, to lean his head upon her breast, to feel that she was consoling him without words, by her pity alone. This longing for pity, for a refuge, was like the last struggle of a soul that will not be content to perish. He bent his head and entered the house without turning again to look at the night.

Terenzio was waiting up for him and followed him to the bedroom, where there was a fire.

'Will the Signor Conte go to bed at once?' he asked.

'No, Terenzio, bring me some tea,' replied his master, sitting down before the fire and stretching out his hands to the blaze.

He was shivering all over with a little nervous tremor.

'The Signor Conte is cold?' asked Terenzio, hastening with affectionate interest to stir up the fire and put on fresh logs.

He was an old servant of the house of Sperelli, having served Andrea's father for many years, and his devotion for the son reached the pitch of idolatry. No human being seemed to him so handsome, so noble, so worthy of devotion. He belonged to that ideal race which furnished faithful retainers to the romance writers of old, but differed from the servants of romance in that he spoke little, never offered advice, and concerned himself with no other business than that of carrying out his master's orders.

'That will do very nicely,' said Andrea, trying to repress the convulsive trembling of his limbs and crouching closer over the fire.

The presence of the old man in this hour of misery and distress moved him singularly. It was an emotion somewhat similar to that which, in the presence of some very kind and sympathetic person, affects a man determined upon suicide. Never before had the old man brought back to him so strongly the recollection of his father, the memory of the beloved dead, his grief for the loss of a great and good friend. Never so much as now had he felt the want of that comforting voice, that paternal hand. What would his father say could he see his son thus crushed under the weight of a nameless distress? How would he have sought to relieve him—what would he have done?

His thoughts turned to the dead father with boundless yearning and regret. And he had not the shadow of a suspicion that in the very teachings of that father lay the primary cause of his wretchedness.

Terenzio brought the tea. He then proceeded slowly to arrange the bed with a care and solicitude that were almost womanly, forgetting nothing, as if he wished to ensure to his master refreshing and unbroken slumbers till the morrow.

Andrea watched him with growing emotion. 'Go to bed now, Terenzio,' he said. 'I shall not want anything more.'

The old man retired and left him alone before the fire—alone with his heart, alone with his misery. Tortured by his inward agitation, he rose and began to pace the room. He was haunted by a vision of Elena, and each time he came as far as the window and turned, he fancied he saw her and started violently. His nerves were in such an overstrung condition that they only increased the disorder of his imagination. The hallucination grew more distinct. He stood still and covered his face with his hands for a moment to control his excitement, and then returned to his seat by the fire.

This time another image rose before him—that of Elena's husband.

He knew him better now. That very evening in a box at the theatre, Elena had introduced them to one another, and he had seized that opportunity to examine him attentively in detail with the keenest curiosity, as though he hoped to obtain some revelation, to draw some secret from him. He could still hear the man's voice—a voice of very peculiar tone, somewhat harsh and strident, with an interrogative inflection at the end of each sentence. Again he saw those pale, pale eyes under the great prominent forehead, eyes that at times assumed a hideous, glassy, dead look, and at others lit up with an indefinable gleam that savoured of madness. Those hands too, he saw—white and smooth and thickly covered with sandy yellow down, and with something obscene in their every movement; their way of raising the opera-glass, of unfolding a handkerchief, of reclining on the cushion in front of the box or turning over the pages of the libretto—hands instinct with vice.

Oh, horror! he saw those hands touching Elena, profaning her with their odious caresses.

The torture became insupportable. He rose once more, went to the window, opened it, shivered under the biting breeze and shook himself. The Trinità de' Monti glittered in the deep blue sky, sharply outlined as if sculptured in faintly tinted marble. Rome, spread out beneath him, had a sheen as of crystal, like a city cut in a glacier.

The calm and sparkling cold brought his mind back to the realities of life and enabled him to recognise the true condition of his mind. He closed the window and sat down again. Once more the enigmatical aspect of Elena's character occupied him, questions crowded in upon him tumultuously, persistently. But he had the strength of mind to co-ordinate them, to attack them one by one, with singular lucidity. The deeper he went in his analysis the more lucid became his mental vision, and he worked out his psychological revenge with cruel relish. At last he felt that he had laid bare a soul, penetrated a mystery. It seemed to him, that thus he made Elena infinitely more his own than in the days of their passion.

What, after all, was this woman?—An unbalanced mind in a sensually inclined body. As with all who are greedy of pleasure, the foundation of her moral being was overweening egotism. Her dominant faculty, her intellectual axis, so to speak, was imagination—an imagination nourished upon a wide range of literature, connected with her sex and perpetually stimulated by neurotic excitement. Possessed of a certain degree of intellectual capacity, brought up in all the luxury of a princely Roman house—that papal luxury which is made up of art and history—she had received a thin coating of æsthetic varnish, had acquired a graceful taste, and, having thoroughly grasped the character of her beauty, sought by skilful simulation and a sapient use of her marked histrionic talents to enhance its spirituality by surrounding it with a delusive halo of ideality.

Into the comedy of human life she thus brought some highly perilous elements, and was thereby the occasion of more ruin and disaster than if she had been a *demi-mondaine* by profession.

Under the glamour of her imagination, every caprice assumed an appearance of pathos. She was the woman of fulminating passions, of suddenly blazing desire. She covered the lusts of the flesh with a mantle of ethereal flame, and could transform into a noble sentiment what was merely a base appetite.

Such was the scathing judgment brought by Andrea against the woman he had once adored. At the root of every action, every expression of Elena's love he now discovered studied artifice, an admirable natural gift for carrying out a pre-arranged scheme, for playing a dramatic part or organising a striking scene. He did not spare their most memorable episodes—neither the first meeting at the Ateletas' dinner, nor the Cardinal Immenraet's sale, nor the ball at the French Embassy, nor the sudden offer of her love in the red room at the Barberini palace, nor their farewells out in the country in the biting March blast. The magic draught which had intoxicated him then now seemed but an insidious poison.

Yet, in spite of it all, certain points perplexed him, as if in penetrating Elena's soul he had penetrated his own, and in the woman's perfidy had seen a reflection of his own. There was much affinity between their two natures. Therefore he *understood*, and little by little, his contempt changed to ironical indulgence. He was so thoroughly conversant with his own mode of procedure.

Then with cold lucidity, he mapped out his plan of campaign. He reviewed every detail of the interview that had taken place on New Year's Eve—more than a week ago—and it pleased him to re-construct the scene, but without the slightest indignation or excitement, only smiling cynically both at Elena and himself. Why had she come?—Simply because this impromptu *tête-à-tête* with a former lover, in the well-known place, after a lapse of two years, had tempted a spirit always on the look-out for fresh emotions, had inflamed her imagination and her curiosity. She thirsted to see into what new situations, new intrigues the dangerous game would lead her. She was perhaps attracted by the novelty of a platonic affection with a person who had already been the object of her sensual passion. As ever, she had thrown herself into the new part with a certain imaginative fervour. Also it was quite possible that, for the moment, she believed what she said, and that this illusory sincerity had furnished her with that deep tenderness of accent, those despairing attitudes, those tears. How well he knew it all! She had a sentimental hallucination as other people have a physical one. She forgot that she was acting a lie, was no longer conscious whether she were living in a world of truth or falsehood, of fiction or reality.

Now this was precisely the moral phenomenon which so constantly took place in himself. Therefore he could not reproach her without injustice. But the discovery very naturally deprived him of the hope of deriving any pleasure from her other than sensual ones. In any case, mistrust would poison all the sweetness of abandon, all soulful rapture. To deceive a confiding and faithful heart, dominate a soul by artifice, possess it wholly and make it vibrate like an instrument—*habere non haberi*—all this, doubtless, gives intense pleasure; but to deceive, and know that one is being deceived in return, is a stupid and fruitless labour, a tiresome and aimless pursuit.

He must therefore work upon Elena to renounce the sisterly scheme and to return to his arms once more. He must regain possession of this beautiful woman, extract the utmost possible pleasure from her beauty and free himself for ever of this passion by reaching the point of satiety. But it was a task demanding prudence and patience. In that first interview, his ardour had availed him nothing. Obviously, she had founded her plan of impeccability on the grand phrase—'Could you endure to share me with another?' The mainspring of the great platonic business was a virtuous horror of divided possession. For the rest, it was just within the bounds of possibility that this horror was not feigned. Most women addicted to the practice of free love, if they do eventually marry, affect, during the early days of their marriage, a savage virtue, and make professions of conjugal fidelity with the most honest determination. Perhaps, therefore, Elena had been affected by this common scruple, in which case, nothing would be more ill-advised than to show his hand too boldly and offend against her new-found virtue. The better plan would be to second her spiritual aspirations, accept her as 'the fondest of sisters, the truest of friends,' intoxicate her with the ideal, be skilfully platonic and then make her glide imperceptibly from frank sisterly relations to a more passionate friendship, and from thence to the complete surrender of her person. In all probability these transitions would occur very rapidly. It all depended upon a wise adjustment of circumstances— —

Thus Andrea Sperelli reasoned, sitting in front of the fire which had glowed upon Elena, laughing among the scattered rose leaves. A boundless lassitude weighed upon him, a lassitude which did not invite sleep, a sense of weariness, so empty, so disconsolate as to be almost a longing for death; while the fire died out on the hearth and the tea grew cold in the cup.

CHAPTER IV

He waited in vain during the days that followed for the promised note to tell him when he might see Elena again——So she did intend to make another appointment with him; the question was—where? At the Casa Zuccari again? Would she risk such an imprudence a second time? This uncertainty kept him on the rack. He passed whole hours in searching for some way of meeting her, of seeing her again. He went several times to the Hotel Quirinal in the hope of being received, but never once did he find her at home. One evening, he saw her again in the theatre with 'Mumps,' as she called her husband. Though only saying the usual things about the music, the singers, the ladies, he infused a supplicating melancholy into his gaze. She seemed greatly taken up by the arrangement of their house. They were going back to the Palazzo Barberini, her old quarters, but were having them much enlarged, and she was for ever occupied with upholsterers and decorators, giving orders and superintending the placing of the furniture.

'Are you going to stay long in Rome?' asked Andrea.

'Yes,' she answered—'Rome will be our winter residence.' Then, after a moment's pause—'You could give us some very good advice about the furniture. Come to the palace one of these days. I am always there from ten to twelve.'

He took advantage of a moment when Lord Heathfield was talking to Giulio Musellaro, who had just entered the box, to say to her, looking her full in the eyes.

'To-morrow?'

'By all means,' she replied with perfect simplicity, as if she had not noticed the tone of his question.

The next morning, about eleven, he set off on foot to the Palazzo Barberini through the Via Sistina. It was a road he had often traversed before—and, for a moment, the impressions of those days seemed to come back to him, and his heart swelled. The fountain of Bernini shone curiously luminous in the sunshine, as if the dolphins and the Triton with his conch-shell had, by some interrupted metamorphose transformed themselves into a more diaphanous material—not stone, nor yet quite crystal. The noise of

the building of new Rome filled all the piazza and the adjoining streets;
country children ran in and out between the carts and horses offering violets
for sale.

As he passed through the gate and entered the garden, he felt that he
was beginning to tremble. 'Then I *do* love her still?' he thought to himself—
'Is she still the woman of *my dreams*?'

He looked at the great palace, radiant under the morning sun, and his
spirit flew back to the days when, in certain chill and misty dawns, this
same palace had assumed for him a look of enchantment. That was in the
early times of his happiness, when he came away warm from her kisses and
full of his new-found bliss; the bells of Trinità de' Monti, of San Isidoro and
the Cappuccini rang out the Angelus into the dawning day, with a muffled
peal as if out of the far distance—at the corner of the street, fires glowed red
round cauldrons of boiling asphalt—a little herd of goats stood against the
white wall of the slumbering house— —

These forgotten sensations rose up once more out of the depths of his
consciousness, and, for an instant, a wave of the old love swept over his
soul, for one moment he tried to imagine that Elena was still the Elena of
those days, that his happiness had endured till now, that none of these
miserable things were true. As he crossed the threshold of the palace, all
this illusory ferment died away on the instant, for Lord Heathfield came
forward to greet him with his habitual and somewhat ambiguous smile.

With that his torture began.

Elena appeared, and shaking hands cordially with him in her husband's
presence, she said—'Bravo, Andrea! Come and help us, come and help us!'

She talked and gesticulated with much vivacity and looked very girlish
in a close-fitting jacket of dark-blue cloth, trimmed round the high collar
and the cuffs with black astrachan and fine black braiding. She kept one
hand in her pocket in a graceful attitude, and with the other pointed out the
various wall-hangings, the pictures, the furniture, asking his advice as to
their most advantageous disposal.

'Where would you put these two chests? Look—Mumps picked them
up at Lucca. These pictures are your beloved Botticelli's.—Where would
you hang these tapestries?'

Andrea recognised the four pieces of tapestry from the Immenraet
sale representing the Story of Narcissus. He looked at Elena, but could
not catch her eye. A profound sense of irritation against her, against her
husband, against all these things took possession of him. He would have
liked to go away, but politeness demanded that he should place his good

taste at the service of the Heathfields; it also obliged him to submit to the archæological erudition of 'Mumps,' who was an ardent collector and was anxious to show him some of his finds. In one cabinet Andrea caught sight of the Pollajuolo helmet, and in another of the rock-crystal goblet which had belonged to Niccolo Niccoli. The presence of that particular goblet in this particular place moved him strangely and sent a flash of mad suspicion through his mind.

So it had fallen into the hands of Lord Heathfield! The famous competition between the Countesses having come to nothing, nobody troubled themselves further about the fate of the goblet, and none of the party had returned to the sale after that day. Their ephemeral zeal had languished and finally died out and passed away, like everything else in the world of fashion, and the goblet had been abandoned to the competition of other collectors. The thing was perfectly natural, but at that moment it appeared to Andrea most extraordinary.

He purposely stopped before the cabinet and gazed long at the precious goblet on which the story of Venus and Anchises glittered as if cut in a pure diamond.

'Niccolo Niccoli!' said Elena, pronouncing the name with an indefinable accent in which the young man seemed to catch a note of sadness.

The husband had just gone into another room to open a cabinet.

'Remember—remember!' murmured Andrea, turning towards her.

'I do remember.'

'Then when may I see you?'

'Ah, when?'

'But you promised me——'

Lord Heathfield returned. They passed on into an adjoining room, making the tour of the apartments. Everywhere they met workmen hanging papers, draping curtains, carrying furniture. Each time Elena asked his opinion, Andrea had to make an effort before answering her, in order to disguise his ill-humour and his impatience. At last, he managed to seize a moment when her husband was occupied with one of the men to say to her in a low voice, unable any longer to conceal his chagrin—

'Why inflict this torture upon me? I expected to find you alone.'

Passing through one of the doors, Elena's hat caught in the portière and was dragged out of place. She laughed and called to Mumps to come and unfasten her veil. And Andrea was forced to look on while those odious hands touched the hair of the woman he desired, ruffling the little curls at the back of her neck, those curls which under his caresses had seemed to breathe out a mysterious perfume, unlike any other, and sweeter and more intoxicating than all the rest.

He hurriedly took his leave under pretext of being due at lunch with some one else.

'We shall move in here on the 1st of February,' Elena said to him, 'and then I hope you will be one of our *habitués*.'

Andrea bowed.

He would have given worlds not to be obliged to touch Lord Heathfield's hand. He went away filled with rancour, jealousy and disgust.

CHAPTER V

At a late hour that same evening, happening to look in at the Club, where he had not been for a long time, whom should he see at one of the card-tables but Don Manuel Ferrès y Capdevila. Andrea greeted him with effusion and inquired after Donna Maria and Delfina—whether they were still at Sienna—when they were coming to Rome.

Don Manuel, who remembered to have won several thousand lire from the young Count during the last evening at Schifanoja, and had recognised in Andrea Sperelli a player of the best form and perfect style, responded with the utmost courtesy and cordiality.

'They have been here some days already; they arrived on Monday,' he answered. 'Maria was much disappointed not to find the Marchesa d'Ateleta in town. I am sure it would give her the greatest pleasure if you would call on her. We are in the Via Nazionale. Here is the exact address.'

He handed one of his cards to Andrea and then returned to the game.

The Duke di Beffi, who was standing with a knot of gentlemen, called Andrea over to them.

'Why did you not come to Cento Celli this morning?' asked the duke.

'I had another appointment,' Andrea replied without reflecting.

'At the Palazzo Barberini perhaps?' said the duke with a shy laugh, in which he was joined by the others.

'Perhaps.'

'Perhaps, indeed?—why, Ludovico saw you go in.'

'And where were you, may I ask?' said Andrea turning to Barbarisi.

'Over the way, at my Aunt Saviano's.'

'Ah!'

'I don't know if you had better luck than we had,' Beffi went on, 'but we had a run of forty-two minutes and got two foxes. The next meet is on Thursday at the Three Fountains.'

'You understand—at the *Three* Fountains, not at the *Four*,' Gino Bomminaco admonished him with comic gravity.

The others burst into a roar of laughter which Andrea could not help joining. He was by no means displeased at their gibes; on the contrary, now that there was no truth in their suspicions, it flattered him for his friends to think he had renewed his relations with Elena. He turned away to speak to Giulio Musellaro, who had just come in. From a few strays words that reached his ear, he found that the group behind him were discussing Lord Heathfield.

'I knew him in London six or seven years ago,' Beffi was saying. 'He was Gentleman of the Bed-chamber to the Prince of Wales as far as I remember——'

The duke lowered his voice, he was evidently retailing the most appalling things. Andrea caught scraps here and there of a highly-spiced nature and, once or twice, the name of a newspaper famous in the annals of London scandal. He longed to hear more; a terrible curiosity took possession of him. His imagination conjured up Lord Heathfield's hands before him— so white, so significant, so expressive, so impossible to forget. Musellaro was still talking, and now said—

'Let us go—I want to tell you——'

On the stairs they encountered Albonico, who was coming up. He was in deep mourning for Donna Ippolita, and Andrea stopped to ask for details of the sad event. He had heard of her death when he was in Paris in November from Guido Montelatici, a cousin of Donna Ippolita.

'Was it really typhus?'

The wan and pale-eyed widower grasped at an occasion for pouring out his griefs, for he made a display of his bereavement as, at one time, he had made a display of his wife's beauty. He stammered and grew lachrymose and his colourless eyes seemed bulging from his head.

Seeing that the widower's elegy threatened to be somewhat long drawn out, Musellaro said to Andrea—

'If we don't take care, we shall be late.'

Andrea accordingly took leave of Albonico, promising to hear the rest of the funeral oration very shortly, and went away with Musellaro.

The meeting with Albonico had re-awakened the singular emotion— partly regret, partly a certain peculiar satisfaction—which he had experienced for several days after hearing the news of this death. The image of Donna Ippolita, half obliterated by his illness and convalescence, by his love for Maria Ferrès, by a variety of incidents, had reappeared to him then as in the dim distance, but invested with a nameless ideality. He had received a promise from her which, though it was never fulfilled, had procured to him the greatest happiness that can befall a man: the victory over a rival, a brilliant victory in the presence of the woman he desired. Later on, between desire and regret another sentiment grew up—the poetic sentiment for beauty idealised by death. It pleased him that the adventure should end thus for ever. This woman who had never been his, but to gain whom he had nearly lost his life, now rose up noble and unsullied before his imagination in all the sublime ideality of death. *Tibi, Hippolyta, semper!*

'But where are we going to?' asked Musellaro, stopping short in the middle of the Piazza de Venezia.

At the bottom of all Andrea's perturbation and all his varying thoughts, was the excitement called up in him by his meeting with Don Manuel Ferrès and the consequent thought of Donna Maria; and now, in the midst of these conflicting emotions, a sort of nervous longing drew him to her house.

'I am going home,' he answered; 'we can go through the Via Nazionale. Come along with me.'

He paid no heed to what his friend was saying. The thought of Maria Ferrès occupied him exclusively. Arrived in front of the theatre, he hesitated a moment, undecided which side of the street he had better take. He would find out the direction of the house by seeing which way the numbers ran.

'What is the matter?' asked Musellaro.

'Nothing—go on,—I am listening.'

He looked at one number and calculated that the house must be on the left hand side, somewhere about the Villa Aldobrandini. The tall pines round the villa looked feathery light against the starry sky. The night was icy but serene; the Torre delle Milizie lifted up its massive bulk, square and sombre among the twinkling stars; the laurels on the wall of Servius slumbered motionless in the gleam of the street lamps.

A few numbers more and they would reach the one mentioned on Don Manuel's card. Andrea trembled as if he expected Donna Maria to appear upon the threshold. He passed so close to the great door that he brushed against it; he could not refrain from looking up at the windows.

'What are you looking at?' asked Musellaro.

'Nothing—give me a cigarette and let us walk a little faster; it is awfully cold.'

They followed the Via Nazionale as far as the Four Fountains in silence. Andrea's preoccupation was patent.

'You must decidedly have something serious on your mind,' said his friend.

Andrea's heart beat so fast that he was on the point of pouring his confidences into his friend's ear, but he restrained himself. Memories of Schifanoja passed across his spirit like an exhilarating perfume, and in the midst of them beamed the figure of Maria Ferrès with a radiance that almost dazzled him. But most distinctly and more luminously than all the rest, he saw that moment in the wood at Vicomile, when she had flung those burning words at him. Would he ever hear such words from her lips again? What had she been doing—what had been her thoughts—how had she spent the days since they parted? His agitation increased with every step. Fragments of scenes passed rapidly before him like the phantasmagoria of a dream—a bit of country, a glimpse of the sea, a flight of steps among the roses, the interior of a room, all the places in which some sentiment had had its birth, round which she had diffused some sweetness, where she had breathed the charm of her person. And he thrilled with profound emotion at the idea that perchance she still carried in her heart that living passion, had perhaps suffered and wept, had dreamed and hoped.

'Well?' said Musellaro, 'and how is your affair with Donna Elena progressing?'

They happened to be just in front of the Palazzo Barberini. Behind the railings and the great stone pillars of the gates stretched the garden, dimly visible through the gloom, animated by the low murmur of the fountains and dominated by the massive white palace where in the portico alone was light.

'What did you say?' asked Andrea.

'I asked how you were getting on with Donna Elena.'

Andrea glanced up at the palace. At that moment he seemed to feel a blank indifference in his heart, the absolute death of desire—the final renunciation.

'I am following your advice. I have not tried to relight the cigarette.'

'And yet, do you know, in this one instance, I believe it would be worth while. Have you noticed her particularly? It seems to me that she has become more beautiful. I cannot help thinking there is something—how shall I express it?—something new, something indescribable about her. No, *new* is not the word. She has gained intensity without losing anything of the peculiar character of her beauty; in short, she is *more Elena* than the Elena of two years ago—the quintessence of herself. It is, most likely, the effect of her second spring, for I should fancy she must be hard on thirty. Don't you think so?'

As he listened, Andrea felt the dull ashes of his love stir and kindle. Nothing revives and excites a man's desire so much as hearing from another the praises of a woman he has loved too long or wooed in vain. A love in its death-throes may thus be prolonged as the result of the envy or the admiration of another; for the disgusted or wearied lover hesitates to abandon what he possesses or is struggling to possess in favour of a possible successor.

'Don't you think so?' Musellaro repeated. 'And, besides, to make a Menelaus of that Heathfield would in itself be an unspeakable satisfaction.'

'So I think,' answered Andrea, forcing himself to adopt his friend's light tone. 'Well, we shall see.'

www.ingramcontent.com/pod-product-compliance
Lightning Source LLC
LaVergne TN
LVHW041440170726
843492LV00008B/2722